P9-ELX-020

YOU CAN DO ANYTHING, DADDY!

MICHAEL REX

G. P. PUTNAM'S SONS

Just for Declan

G. P. PUTNAM'S SONS
A division of Penguin Young Readers Group. Published by The Penguin Group.
Penguin Group (USA) Inc., 375 Hudson Street, New York, NY 10014, U.S.A.
Penguin Group (Canada), 90 Eglinton Avenue East, Suite 700, Toronto, Ontario, Canada M4P 2Y3 (a division of Pearson Penguin Canada Inc.). Penguin Books Ltd, 80 Strand, London WC2R 0RL, England. Penguin Ireland, 25 St. Stephen's Green, Dublin 2, Ireland (a division of Penguin Books Ltd.). Penguin Group (Australia), 250 Camberwell Road, Camberwell, Victoria 3124, Australia (a division of Pearson Australia Group Pty Ltd). Penguin Books India Pvt Ltd, 11 Community Centre, Panchsheel Park, New Delhi - 110 017, India. Penguin Group (NZ), Cnr Airborne and Rosedale Roads, Albany, Auckland 1310, New Zealand (a division of Pearson New Zealand Ltd). Penguin Books (South Africa) (Pty) Ltd, 24 Sturdee Avenue, Rosebank, Johannesburg 2196, South Africa. Penguin Books Ltd, Registered Offices: 80 Strand, London WC2R 0RL, England.

Manufactured in China by South China Printing Co. Ltd. Design by Gunta Alexander. Text set in Minister.

Library of Congress Cataloging-in-Publication Data
Rex, Michael. You can do anything, daddy! / Michael Rex. p. cm. Summary: After receiving assurances that his father would save him from increasingly dangerous and scary pirates, a boy reassures his father in return. [1. Fathers and sons—Fiction. 2. Imagination—Fiction. 3. Pirates—Fiction.] I. Title. PZ7.R32875You 2007 [Fic]—dc22 2006008253 ISBN 978-0-399-24298-4
10 9 8 7 6 5 4 3 2 1 First Impression

"Daddy, if I got taken by pirates,
would you save me?"

YE SEA

"Of course, Son."

"What if they had a boat?"

"I would swim after them."

"What if there were sharks in the water?"

"I would build my own boat and chase them."

"Daddy, would you chase them
if they were gorilla pirates?"
"Absolutely."

"What if they took me in the jungle?"

"I would cut a path right through the bush."

"What if there were tigers in the bush?"

“I would swing from the trees to follow you.”

"Daddy, would you follow me
if they were robot gorilla pirates?"
"Without a doubt."

"What if they took me in some dark caves?"

"I would light a torch and go right in."

"What if there were snakes in the caves?"

"I would tie them in knots and run after you."

"Daddy, would you run after me
if they were robot gorilla pirates
from Mars?"

"Certainly."

"What if they took me up a high cliff?"

"I would put on my boots and climb up."

"What if there were vultures on the cliffs?"

“I would pluck their feathers and
come to get you.”

"Daddy, what if they were going to
put me in a rocket and
send me into space?"

"Then I would make them STOP."

"How, Daddy?"

"I would shout: 'Hey, Robot Gorilla Pirates from Mars! Look at this!' Then I would hypnotize them with my shiny gold watch, and I'd throw it over the cliff!"

"They would put you down and jump right after it!"

"Then they'd sink to the bottom of the ocean.

All pirates are fools for gold!"

"Thanks for saving me. You can do anything, Daddy!"
"Anything for you, Son."

"Daddy, after saving me,
would you be hot and thirsty?"
"Of course."

"Then I would give you some cold apple juice."

"Mmmm, that's good."

"Daddy, would you have scrapes and scratches?"

"Absolutely."

"Then I would put medicine and bandages on them."

"Ahhh, they feel better already."

"Daddy, would you have bumps and bruises?"
"Certainly."
"Then I would kiss them and make them better."
"Thanks for fixing me up, Son."

"Anything for you, Daddy."